DIARY

of a
Legendary Iron Golem & His Pig

VOLUME 1

Christopher Craft

Welcome

Minecraft has changed a lot since the war between pigs and humans. Pigs can talk and craft and build, and everyone is a vegetarian. Well, everyone except for the gang of wolves that attack the pig's village. Jon the pig has only a few days to find help for the pigs that were captured in the wolf invasion before they have their annual midnight feast. Bernard might be the kindest iron Golem in the entire human village, but for some reason, people are afraid of a ten foot tall metal monster. Bernard thinks he might never find a friend until he meets Jon. Together, they must save the pig village.

Fiction Disclaimer

This is a work of fiction. Names, characters, businesses, places, events and incidents are either the products of the author's imagination or used in a fictitious manner. Any resemblance to actual persons, living or dead, or actual events is purely coincidental.

Copyright ©
Christopher Craft 2015

Thank you!

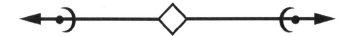

TABLE OF CONTENTS

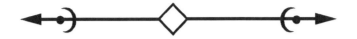

1.

PIG – A PIG NAMED JON

RIGHT ABOUT NOW, I'M PROBABLY FLEEING FOR MY life away from my friends and family. Well, not away from them exactly, I'm actually running away from the wolves. Now, I know that you might think, "Why don't you just pull out a sword and play whack-a-doggie with the business end?" The issue with that is, I don't exactly have hands to pick the sword up. Pigs usually don't.

Again, my incredible powers of deduction are telling me what your next question is, "If you don't have hands, how can you write in a journal, or even hold a pencil?" That's not important right now. Here's what is. My name is Jon, I'm a pig from a village called Broom, and everyone I know is in danger. How did this happen, you might wonder? Well, for once, I'm glad you asked.

Like I said, Broom is a village of pigs. We're not the typical barnyard sort you see and (gasp!) eat from time to time. No, we're different. For one thing, we can talk. We can also dig, and build, and craft. Because of this, we've been the envy of every other mob in Minecraft, including some of the monsters. Normally, they don't try anything, but for some reason, the wolves got together and decided to knock us down a pig... I mean peg. They attacked in the middle of the night, and rounded us all up in the center of town. We did our best to fight them off, but there were so many of them, and they were so strong, we eventually had to give in. But not before they made us go back to our homes and gather supplies for the trek up the mountain that the village sits on. Luckily enough, they didn't do a very good job supervising us, and a large group of us gathered some weapons and tried to stop them. Before the fighting broke out, I had my little sister Hazel go hide down in the basement of our home. Our house was built directly into the side of a hill, and if you didn't already know where it was, you could never find it, or at least that's what I hoped. After that, I and the rest of the freedom fighters tried our best to defeat the wolves, but they just kept coming. We were outmatched. We might have been smarter, but they were stronger and faster. We didn't stand a chance. Before we captured though, we found an exit through a ravine. There was a small bridge, only a single block wide. Those wild wolves couldn't do a thing except watch us walk across and to the other side. We were safe, but there were still a lot of pigs left in the village, like the elderly or the young or... my sister. So here I am, walking along a well worn trail on my way to the next village over to find some help. Sadly though, this village wasn't made up of our piggy brethren. It was human.

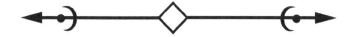

2.

IRON GOLEM – AN IRON GOLEM NAMED BERNARD.

MY NAME IS BERNARD. THE HUMANS IN THE VILLAGE call me an iron Golem, on account of the fact that I'm made of iron and I'm a Golem. I spawned beside the mayor's house in the morning time. When he woke up, he saw me standing at his door. When he fainted, it took two hours for him to wake up. I tried offering him my poppy flower, but when humans are unconscious they aren't very good at accepting gifts.

That reminds me, I forgot to talk about my flower. My flower is the most important thing I own. Actually, it's the only thing I own. One day, when I find someone who I can call my friend, I will give that person my poppy flower. So far, I haven't found anyone like that.

Part of the trouble of being a ten foot giant who is made out of iron is that you make people a bit uneasy. One time, when I was on my normal nightly patrol, a couple came by and I waved at them. They must have thought I was shooing them, because they ran away screaming and never looked back. I didn't see them again for a while, but when I did, they didn't look at me. I don't know how they didn't see me, but I guess they didn't.

It also seems odd to me that so many people would be afraid of an iron Golem when so many other Golems patrol the streets of the village at night with me. I mean, we aren't all out at once, but there are about ten of us altogether. You'd think they'd be used to us by now, but you'd be wrong if you thought that.

Anyway, I can't really think of a way to end

my first journal entry, so I thought I'd write down a conversation I heard in an alley way while I was patrolling last night. I didn't catch the beginning part, but they seemed worried by the time I heard the middle part. I don't think they saw me, so this might be a secret, but that's why I'm writing it in my journal, because no one will ever know.

"Yeah Mark, they took out the whole village, or at least that's what I heard. I mean, no one's been up there yet, but from our closest outposts there, the wolves took about one third of them captive and brought the little pink critters to the top of the mountain."

"You mean all those poor pigs are trapped? Did the wolves... you know... eat them?"

"No! Of course they didn't. Wolves can only eat during a full moon, it's just this odd rule they have. Although, the next full moon is pretty soon if I have my moon cycle memorized correctly."

"Gee, why don't we go do something to help them? Maybe the mayor could send the police!"

"Mark, don't be silly. If those wolves captured a whole village, what are a few measly cops with stone swords going to do? Nothing, that's what, anyway, how's the wife and kids?"

That was the conversation. I walked away after that. I don't know exactly what they're talking about, but I really do feel sorry for the pigs. Okay, I'm done for now. Bye.

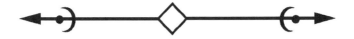

3.

PIG – WHAT EVEN IS THAT?!

I WALKED FOR WHAT FELT LIKE DAYS, BUT THEY WERE probably only a couple of hours. My legs are short and stubby, so I tire easily. When I arrived at the human village, it was just after dusk. The street torches had come on, but the sun was still out just enough that you didn't really need them. I was sleepy, exhausted, hungry, and thirsty all at once. Before I could do anything, I'd need to replenish my vitals.

Oh, one more thing I should mention about pigs before I continue. It's a little bit of a history lesson, and you've probably heard it already, but don't worry, it'll still be interesting. I mean, it is about pigs, after all.

A long time ago, but not so long that my great grand pig couldn't remember it, there was a war between pigs and humans. Apparently, humans had been eating us just because we couldn't talk. We finally got fed up with it (not like them, a different kind of fed) and decided to hold a revolution. The Pig Revolutionary War lasted a year. It would have lasted a lot longer if it hadn't been for a certain pig and a certain human coming together in peace. They learned each other's ways, and eventually, languages. They became the best of friends, and were the ambassadors for each of the factions. There was a long period of debating and fighting that was off the battlefield, but eventually, there was an agreement. Pigs and humans were to be treated equally, and that meant that humans had to stop chowing down on pigs, and in fact, all of humanity became vegetarian.

I only felt the need to say that because, in the old days, a pig deciding to just waltz through the middle of any human settlement was not a good idea, but now, it was almost commonplace. That's why it came as a little bit of a surprise that every human I made eye contact with would stare at me just a little too long. I guess the word of what happened to the one and only pig village had already gotten around.

I was heading up a side road, when I felt a slight tremor in the ground. Earthquakes were rare, but not unheard of. I dismissed it quickly enough though, because the smell of freshly crafted bread was wafting through the air and hitting my nose right in the bulls-eye. My mouth was watering by the time I hopped up on a seat and a short human, maybe a child, walked over and took my order.

"Yes, I'd like all the water and bread you can bring me for this much money." I said, holding up a little coin. The kid smiled at me.

"I'll be right back with your order!" He said cheerfully, and I decided to look out the window at the city around me. I loved people watching. This particular person watching

escapade wasn't going exactly as I'd hoped it would.

It was fully dark, and out of the darkness walked the largest creature I'd ever seen. It was huge and shiny and silver, with vines growing on it, making it seem ancient and brand new all at the same time. It was carrying a small red flower in its hands with a surprisingly delicate grip. I was about to say something, but the little boy stepped between me and my view of the creature outside. He had a bucket of water and two loaves of bread on the table in front of me before I snapped out of my daze.

"You saw that thing too, right? I'm not just hallucinating from dehydration?" I asked, gulping down the water, hoping that the image of the creature would leave my mind if I drank enough to stop being crazy.

"Oh, you mean the iron Golem? Yeah, they can be pretty scary... I mean, I avoid them at all costs; I even go the long way home from here so I don't have to look one in the eyes. But don't worry, they aren't dangerous. They spawn in the village and protect us from the monsters at night. I think I remember that pig villages don't spawn them... well, I guess the pig village isn't spawning much of anything anymore..." Then the little boy looked up, and his face became extremely apologetic and remorseful. "Oh my goodness, I didn't mean that! I just, well, we've all heard the news about your village, I just thought... I'm so sorry." He said, and he was being genuine, so I forgave him. I finished chewing the last piece of bread that I had in my mouth and then spoke.

"It's okay. I understand. Hey, can you do me a favor though? Can you point me in the direction of the mayor's office? I need to speak with him right away." I said, giving the boy a reassuring smile. It was time to do what I came here to do. It was time to save my sister.

I approached the mayor's office, careful to avoid the gaze of the monstrous iron Golems. I know the boy said they were harmless, but they kind of made that hard to believe. I nudged open the main door with my snout, and walked into the lobby.

"Hello, my name is Jon. I need to speak with Mayor Steve right away." I said to a receptionist. There was a wooden sign on his desk that said Herman.

"Do you have an appointment? I can't let you see him without an appointment. Mayor Steve is quite the busy guy, and it's quite late. I

can pencil you in for a meeting around noon tomorrow, if that's a good time for you. How about it?" Herman said. I was a little angry. Of course the government was the last to know anything important.

"I'm from the pig village to the west called Broom, you may have heard of it. Right now, it has been reduced to rubble, and most of my people are being led up to a cave in a mountain where they will be eaten in less than a week unless I can convince Mayor Steve to help me stop it. Do I need an appointment now, Herman?" I said, with a little too much edge in my voice. I shouldn't have been so severe with the guy, he was just doing his job, but right now, I needed to speak with Steve, and there was no time for manners.

"S-sure thing Jon. Just go down that hall and it will be the first door on your right. Sorry to keep you waiting." Herman said, and he was absolutely shaken. I made a mental note to apologize on my way out, but headed down to Steve's office without another word.

"Hello there. I know why you've come. There's no need for formalities, what can I do to help?" Steve asked. Steve was the original founder of this human village, and he'd been elected mayor every year since. He was old and gray now though, his teal shirt was faded and torn, but he was still a proud and dignified looking human none the less.

"Well, I think we'll need nothing short of a small army. These wolves weren't like ordinary wolves. They were organized. They aren't individually all that bright, but when they are working in a pack, they are a force to be reckoned with. I think about twenty or so of your best military police armed with iron swords and armor should be enough to at least free the majority of my village, and then after that, we can all regroup and go in for a mass invasion, and take back the land bit by bit." I said. I had plenty of time to think about it on the way here, and after fighting the wolves myself, it seemed like the only thing that might actually break their defenses.

"No." Steve said his expression blank. It took me a minute to register what he said.

"Wait, what do you mean no? How can you say that?" I said, more than a little distraught. Steve was supposed to be a knight in shining armor that would swoop in and save the day, now he was just telling me no.

"Let me explain. As you may have noticed while coming into town, we have patrols of those large creatures, we call them iron Golems. Whenever an aggressive mob comes close to the village, the iron Golems attack them. We haven't had a need for any kind of military for quite some time. In fact, as far as police go, we only have five people who are actually trained. And as for equipment, they use stone swords and no armor. It's been so long since we needed to protect ourselves from a threat that we've nearly forgotten how. So no, I can't help you, and for that I am truly sorry." Steve said. His face showed genuine sympathy. It made sense, but that didn't change the fact that I needed help. I thought about what he said, and I got an idea.

"What about the iron Golems? I noticed only about three of them were actually patrolling, and I've heard that there are as many as twelve of them spawned. Even just two or three of those guys would be enough to bust up the wolves' defenses." I said.

Yes, you're probably right. They are truly resilient creatures, and I'd be more than happy for some of them to accompany you back to your village and help free the captives and take back your land, but the thing is, it's not up to me. The iron Golems don't answer to anyone, in fact, we're not even sure if they talk at all. They worked out the patrol rotation all by themselves, and we've never seen one leave the village for any reason. I'll tell you what though, if you can convince the iron Golems to follow you into battle, then I will pardon them of their duty." Steve said. I thought about it for a moment, and then smiled.

"Great! Is there anything you do know about them that might help me out?" I asked. Steve looked thoughtful, and then spoke.

"Yes. They sleep during the day. So if you want to get a chance to talk to one, it would be now." Steve yawned loudly, and that reminded me of how absolutely exhausted I was. "As for me, I'm going to bed. I wish you the best of luck." Steve said with finality, and I took that as a sign that I should be leaving. I walked out to the village street, and there was almost no one out, no one except for a certain red flower holing iron Golem, of course.

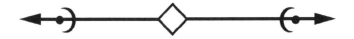

4.

Iron Golem – Is this friendship or a concussion?

I WOKE UP THAT NIGHT FEELING ALL MIXED UP. I FELT like something really good might happen and like something really bad might happen. I was both happy and sad in equal amounts. It was confusing, and odd, and... all mixed up.

That didn't matter as much to me though once I ate breakfast. Today was the day that the baker crafted his bread, so I could smell it coming long before I saw it. A young human walked over with a mine cart filled to the brim with loaves of bread and buckets of water. I moaned a thank you as best I could, but he just ran away again. I needed to keep practicing, I almost had it. Or maybe that's just how people react to being thanked. I still had a lot to learn about humans.

Tonight was my night to go on patrol around the city. I was supposed to walk around the shops and town hall, so I would get to visit the place where I spawned, which was nice. Maybe that was the good thing that was going to happen. I hoped I wouldn't find out about the bad.

I ate up the bread and drank all the buckets of water in a hurry. I wanted to get an early start, because there would still be a few people in the streets. I loved watching the people as they walked by, even if they were walking quickly away from me. I liked to day dream that one of them might be my friend, but we never really get to hang out, me being a ten foot tall iron Golem and all.

My first pass by of the night was the local bakery. I especially loved this part because I'd get to get a good whiff of the fresh bread again. It was one of my favorite smells. As I walked by, I took a sniff of my poppy flower, just to remind it that I liked the way it smelled the most. When I walked by, I caught the gaze of a small pink person. He didn't look like a person except for the eyes. He was scared of me, just like normal people. Then, the young human baker from before stepped between the little pink thing and I before it could run away screaming. It was almost like he didn't want to run away at all... almost.

I spend a good bit of the night just wandering around the outskirts of town looking into the darkness of the forest and fields, searching for any signs of monsters. I was really good at that. The other iron Golems said that I had the best night vision out of any of them. All the iron Golems rarely spoke to each other, so the compliment meant all the more. I walked around like that for a while before I headed for my final destination of the night, town hall.

The town hall was where all the human leaders would meet up every day and talk and then leave. I don't quite understand what they talk about, but they make it seem important. The largest building in all of the town hall is the mayor's office. He is the most important human leader of all. He's basically the boss. I've never seen him walking around town, so I think he stays busy all the time. I guess that means he works hard at leading the people.

I passed by his building, and heard a small squeal, but decided not to waste my time turning and looking at who it was. Generally when people make those noises, it means they are already scared enough and it's better that I just leave them alone. I kept on walking along the outskirts of town hall, when I saw something in the distance, something green. The closer it got, the more I realized what it was. It was a creeper!

Creepers were the worst of the worst. When they blow up, they take everything with them. I had an almost-friend named Gregory who was an iron Golem. He was blown up with a creeper, and his poppy flower went with him. I needed to be careful with this green guy, or I'd be done for.

When I charged forward, I could hear a yelp from behind me. It was the same voice that squealed before, but now I was in fighting mode, there was no time to turn and look. I made contact with the creeper in a field that was just at the village's outer limits. If it blew up here, everyone would still be safe. I swung up

at it, and it flew high up in the air. It made a sizzling noise, and began to flash a bright white. Creepers were tricky monsters. Sometimes, they faked out, and they wouldn't explode when they flashed. But, I was so close to the village now that if I backed up and it didn't explode, it would be in range of the buildings and people. I couldn't let that happen. As the creeper came down, the flashing started to pulse faster. I lifted both of my hands in the air, and waited for him to be close enough. As soon as I knew I could hit him, I swung both my fists at the creeper in an attempt to knock it out into the woods to explode. Almost immediately after it started sailing backwards through the air though, it blew up.

Luckily it was far enough away from all the buildings that no one was hurt. Sadly, I found out what my bad feeling was about. I was launched backwards by the force of the explosion, and I could only hear a ringing in my ears. Dirt blocks were flying everywhere, and I landed with a hard thud. I think I became unconscious for a little while, and I could see why the mayor couldn't accept my flower when I spawned. I was asleep for a long time, because when I woke up, it was almost morning. I was in the doctor's office, and there was a golden apple sitting on the book shelf beside me. I sat up, and my head nearly touched the ceiling. They had to knock down an entire wall of the building in order to fit me in here, so I could hear the doctor arguing with a man outside. I sat and ate my golden apple, feeling better and better as I ate it, but feeling worse and worse as I continued to listen to their conversation. I wrote it down even though it made me sad.

"I'm telling you doctor, these so called guardians are nothing by trouble! He took out my entire carrot patch with that creeper! I bet he even did it on purpose!"

"Now listen here, he did away with the monster like he was meant to, maybe you should have put your carrot patch a little closer to the city and a little further from the blast zone! Besides, nobody got hurt, and that's the important thing."

"Yeah yeah, I guess you're right. Well, I need to get back, those carrots won't replant themselves."

And that was it. Nobody got hurt. Except that that's not true, because I was hurt. Did they think of me as nobody? Did I not matter?

I crawled out of the doctor's office and began walking quickly towards the iron Golem cabins that were just outside of town. I needed to sleep. I was wrong this morning, the good feeling was wrong, this whole night was wrong. As I walked along, I looked at the humans in a new way. Each time they looked away from me, or stared at me, or looked at me like I was a monster, I realized that I wasn't the monster here, they were. I protected them and guarded the village almost every night since I spawned and yet they still thought of me as nothing. I never once thought of them as nothing, and that's what made me sad. I knew they were something worthwhile, why couldn't they see that in me?

Then, I heard it again, that same squeaky, small voice from before. This time, I had nowhere to be, and a lot of time to get there, so I turned. At first I didn't see anyone, but then I looked even further down. There, with its head only just barely rising above my knee was that pink thing from the bakery. This time though, its eyes weren't filled with fear. Instead, they were friendly and kind. I'd only seen other humans look at each other that way; they'd never looked at me like that. But here was one, even if it was small and pink.

"Hey! I don't know if you remember me... I was there when, well, you know. Boom. Anyway, I wanted to ask if you were okay. You took a pretty hard hit there, big guy." The little pink human smiled at me. I smiled back.

"He listen, my name's Jon. I'm from the pig village to the west of here. I had a favor to ask you." Then Jon yawned loudly, almost as loud as my growls. "Sorry, I should actually get some rest first. You wouldn't happen to know of a good place to catch some sleep, would you? Like an inn or something?" Jon asked. I'd never really been talked to so directly by a human... or a pig, I guess. I don't understand the

difference, but I think Jon said he was a pig. The only place I could think of was the iron Golem cottages. I nodded at Jon, and turned on my heel. I could hear him following behind. I slowed down a lot because his little legs had to move so fast that he was almost in a full sprint just to keep up with my walk. Eventually, I found a pace that he could keep up with.

"So, where are we going?" Jon asked. I tried to tell him we were going home, but all I could get out was an odd throaty sound. I looked down at Jon, and he was shocked. At first I thought it was fear, but no, it was definitely shock.

"Did you just say home? You can talk?" Jon asked excitedly. I couldn't believe he had understood me! I didn't want to mess it up by trying a word I hadn't practiced, so instead I just nodded. Jon looked quite pleased.

We only walked for a little while after that until we got to the iron Golem cottages. I showed Jon my bed, and then put my hands together and placed them on my face like a pillow to tell him I wanted to go to bed.

"Oh yeah, sure thing, I need some shut eye too. Good night... or is it good day? Anyway, I'll see you when the sun's down. I'll just go out here to sleep. I like the feeling of the soft cool dirt on my belly when I sleep." Jon said, and then he trotted away and out the cottage door.

I lay down and thought about the day's events. The bad feeling had turned out to be really bad, but the good feeling had turned out to be even better. I twisted the red poppy flower in my hand and thought that maybe, just maybe, I had made a friend.

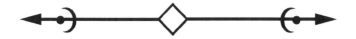

5.

PIG – THE POPPY FLOWER

WHEN I WOKE UP, I WAS STILL GROGGY AND
TIRED. I'D been tossing and turning all
night because of bad dreams. I dreamt that I
had convinced the iron Golem to go and rescue
hazel, but when he got there, the wolves
surrounded him. He fought valiantly, but one of
the wolves bit down hard on the poppy flower
in his hand, ripping away most of the petals.
After that, the iron Golem seemed to be
fighting an uphill battle. He was weak and
weary by the end, and the wolves overwhelmed

him with sheer numbers.

So, with that still fresh on my mind, I awoke to see the big lug standing directly over me. I have to say, it took all of my self control to keep it together. The iron Golem was a scary looking creature. He seemed to be kind though, so I had no reason to be afraid. I smiled and nodded at him, and then stood up and stretched all four legs one by one.

"Good morning, well, good afternoon." I said, noticing that the sun was going down, not coming up. Iron Golems were nocturnal, and that meant that if I wanted to convince this particular iron Golem to help me, I'd have to start being nocturnal too.

"You know, we met so abruptly last night that I never got a chance to ask you what your name was. My name's Jon, and you?" I asked. The iron Golem looked puzzled for a moment, and then walked over to a small gathering of trees. They were newly planted birch trees, and so they were shorter than the forest around them. The iron Golem grabbed one of the

smallest ones in the middle and pulled up, yanking it out of the dirt. He then walked over to a clearing of dirt that wasn't covered in grass and began to write with the tree as if it were a pencil. When he was finished, he had actually written a word!

"Bernard? Your name is Bernard?" I asked. He nodded. "Where did you learn to write?" I asked. As far as I knew, I was the first person to know that iron Golems were just creatures, but people, that they were smart enough to communicate in words, so who taught an iron Golem to write? It'd be like trying to teach a magma cube or a rabbit.

Bernard looked over at a small building towards town, and then pointed. I looked over at it. There were no children in sight, but my guess was that the building was actually a school. There was a small window in the back.

"So you sat there during the day and learned about the human's language?" I asked. Bernard smiled wide with pride. I was impressed. Bernard then used his massive feet to clear the dirt and smooth it out so he could write something else. Using the birch tree, he began our conversation.

"What is a pig?" He asked. I realized that he'd probably never seen or maybe even heard of a pig before since he never left the village.

"I'm sort of like a human, but I'm not. I and

the rest of my village are all pigs, pink and four legged people. We read and write just like the humans in this village do. Actually, we do most things like the humans in this village do. Well, that is, we used to…" I trailed off. It was painful talking about the village I had to leave behind. When I came to the human village, I had thought that scaring off the wolves would be as easy as asking Mayor Steve, but now there was actually a chance that I might not be able to rescue them after all. Bernard flattened the dirt and then wrote again.

"Used to?" he asked. After that, I unloaded my story. I told him all about the evil wolves coming and taking over my village, I told him about our struggle to fight back that inevitably blew up in our faces, and finally, I told him about my sister, Hazel.

"She's being held up there and can't leave. I'd thought that she was safe in our house, but now I don't know anymore. The wolves are going to eat up all of the pigs that they've taken captive, almost a third of my village, and maybe my sister was found and they'd…

they'd..." I tried finishing my sentence, but I just couldn't. The thought of those dirty wolves taking a bite out of Hazel was just too much for me to deal with. Again, Bernard cleared the dirt and wrote another message, but this time, he wrote it slowly, but I think he wrote it slowly on purpose. It was like he wanted me to understand that he meant it.

"They will not hurt pigs. I will help you stop them." Bernard said. I couldn't believe my little pink ears. I didn't even have to ask. But then I thought about it for a moment.

"Will the other iron Golems come with us?" I asked. This time, Bernard shook his head no. He wrote something else in the dirt.

"Their poppies are still theirs. They can't leave the village." He said. He held out the little red flower in his hand, and let it bathe in the moonlight around us. For whatever reason, the other iron Golems couldn't leave if they still owned their poppy flowers. I couldn't get an army of humans, and now I can't even get a squad of iron Golems.

"What's so special about not owning the

flowers? Why can't they just give them to some of the villagers here and then roam free?" I asked. It wasn't making any sense. Apparently, this was something that Bernard had already known I was going to ask, because even while I was still asking it, he was already finished writing his response in the sand.

"The flowers are us. We have to give them to a friend who will protect them from harm, and we are strongest when the flowers are close." He said. I remembered back to my dream, and how powerful Bernard seemed until his flower was destroyed. After that he was weaker than... than me.

"Well who protects your flower?" I asked. They'd need to come along too, because if the flower would make Bernard even stronger, he might be able to take out the wolves by himself. There was still a chance for Hazel, for the village. Bernard lifted up the hand that his flower was not in, and brought it towards me slowly. He then held out a finger, and tapped me on the chest. He then dropped the flower from out of his hand, and I had no choice but to catch it in my mouth. I placed it down on the ground slowly, and then looked back up at Bernard, who had a grin, the same one he had yesterday outside of the doctor's office. He considered me a friend.

"Me? But Bernard, I don't even have hands! How am I supposed to protect the flower?" I asked. Bernard pointed towards the cottage. The other iron Golems had woken up while we were talking. The one's who were on patrol were gone, but there was still about six iron Golems just walking and socializing with each other. There was one that was alone though. It had a small silver piece of metal in its hand.

Bernard began to walk over towards the lone iron Golem, and I followed closely behind. When we had made out way all the way over to him, the iron Golem had a small replica of a poppy flower in his hand made out of the metal piece he had been working with. He was a sculptor.

Bernard looked at him and made some grunting noises. They were talking. Then the other iron Golem began to make a thunderous booming sound that shook the ground beneath my feet. I thought he was angry, or screaming, but he was actually laughing. Then, the sculptor picked up a thin piece of metal from a pile beside him and began to work.

I still have no idea how he used his fingers that were bigger than my head to craft something so delicate and ornate, but he did it. He presented me with a pendant he had made out of iron. He used a small bit of woven grass rope as a chord and placed it around my neck. He then reached down and demonstrated that there was a panel on the front that could open and close. I got the message, and put the small delicate red poppy flower into the metallic box and closed the lid. Instantly Bernard let out a breath of relief, and I did too.

"Thank you for the gift sculptor!" I said as Bernard and I walked back to the dirt clearing. Bernard picked the tree trunk up again and began to write once more.

"Now we go. Now we save them. Hop up." He said. I was happy and puzzled at the same time.

"Hop up?" I asked. In response, he bent

down and tapped his left shoulder. I climbed up until I was in position, and then when he stood up, I was perched on his shoulder. I felt like I was on top of a house, but that wasn't right. The roofs of the houses were lower.

Bernard began walking to the west, leaving the way I had come. I travelled to this human village in hopes that I would find people to help free my village from tyranny. What I got wasn't military police. It was something that I hoped would prove much more useful. I got a flower. More importantly, I got a friend.

I held on tightly as Bernard picked up his pace. I felt like I was flying. The wind was so loud in my ears I couldn't even hear myself think, so instead I spoke. My voice was just barely audible, and most of it was carried away with the wind, but my words rang true.

"I'm... no, we're coming to save you Hazel. Just hold on." Yet even as I said that, I looked up at the moon and noticed something unsettling. It was almost full. The table was almost set. Dinner was nearly ready. Hazel was on the menu.

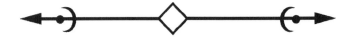

6.

Iron Golem – Stand Together, or Not at All

I HAD BEEN WALKING FOR A WHILE ON THE PRAIRIE. It was nearly day time again, and I was getting sleepy. Jon was still awake, but I could tell that he was nodding off to sleep as well. He was holding the metal box that Gunter made him tightly in the cradle of his arm. I picked a good person to hold on to it for me, that's for sure.

I noticed that there weren't many monsters roaming around. I hoped that was because they were all busy somewhere else. Maybe they decided to take a night off. I was still shaken up about the explosion, and running into another creeper was the last thing I wanted to do, especially since I was so tired.

I would normally have been asleep by now if I were back at the village. I looked up at the sky. Jon had told me that the wolves would eat up the other pigs when it was full. To me it already looked full, but Jon explained that it still had a tiny sliver left that was still dark. I really hope that he is right, because I don't think he'll be my friend if I let his village get eaten. I am an iron Golem, after all. We know from the day we spawn that protecting people is our mission. Sometimes the mission is hard, especially at the human village where no one ever thanks you or tells you that you did a good job. Jon says that it is because they don't know that I can understand them, but I'm not sure.

I looked in the distance and could see the outline of the mountain. Jon's village was somewhere over there, but the mountain was still really far away. Suddenly, I heard something whistle by my head. I turned and saw what it was. On the ground behind me was an arrow. I heard the whistling again and knew that I was under fire.

"Bernard, take cover behind that hill, I see them!" Jon shouted at me as an arrow whizzed by his head, barely missing him and scraping my shoulder. I ran as quickly as I could behind the large dirt hill, and I could hear the rattle of bones as the skeletal archers approached.

"Did you get hit?" Jon asked urgently. I shook my head. "Good. There are two of them over there. I knew it would be too easy to get all the way there without encountering any monsters. So, what do you want to do? Should we fight or run?" Jon asked, pulling out a stone shovel and gripping it in his jaw. I did my best to try and tell him what I wanted to do, but the words were awkward and slow.

"I will fight. Jon will not." I said. It took me a few seconds to get all of that out. By that time, the skeletons were on us. I think Jon got the message though.

I broke out into a sprint around the hill and

then dug my feet into the dirt. The skeletons charged me. They both had an arrow ready to fire in their bow. They let go of the bow's string and the arrows soared quickly toward me. Swiped at them with my arm, and knocked them out of the air. My skin was made of metal, so I didn't feel much. I turned my head and checked to be sure Jon was okay. He was holding on to my shoulder for dear life, and he was probably scared witless that I let the arrows get that close, but he was fine.

I charged at the first skeleton and was on him before he could load another arrow. I slung my arm at him, and he flew back and into the tall grass. I probably got him, but I made sure that I didn't get too comfortable turning my back on the grass. The next skeleton wasn't as easily beaten. I tried to swing my other arm at him, but her rolled out of the way and launched another arrow at me, this time aiming for my neck. Sadly, Jon was in the way, otherwise I would have just let the arrow shatter against my neck and gone in for my next attack. Instead, I flung my hand up as a shield and the arrow hit my fingers. My whole body was made of metal, but there were certain sections that were made of stronger stuff than the others. I bellowed in pain when the arrow made contact. It shattered like the other had, but it also hurt my hand pretty badly. Now I was angry.

I launched a counterattack almost immediately. The skeleton tried dodging, but I was prepared for that. I threw out my arms at last minute like a net and caught him in my arm. I then flung him over to the grass as well, but this time I was certain that I had gotten him. I stayed still for a moment to listen and see if we were still in danger, but I think we were okay. At least, I hoped we were.

"Wow Bernard, you saved my life back there. I would have been a goner if you hadn't stopped that arrow!" Jon exclaimed with a smile. I smiled too, because I knew it was true. I saved my friend. I was really proud.

After that, we kept on walking, not even stopping when the sun came up. When we were close enough to make out individual blocks in the mountain, Jon had me change directions.

"Go that way Bernard. When I left to go get help from the humans, I wasn't the only one who had escaped the wolves. Actually, more than half of the village escaped. I was supposed to be getting reinforcements to help with our rebellion. We pigs might be small, but we're strong. We already have warriors, we just needed back up. And now we've got something better than an army, we've got you." Jon said. I smiled at that. I'm glad I do not have to fight this battle alone. I couldn't protect Jon from all the wolves.

I made the turn that he suggested, and away we went. Basically, I was just circling around the base of the mountain, but it was a lot trickier than it sounds because of the canyons and cliffs. It was an odd landscape. I'd walk along for a while, and then Jon would tell me to stop walking, and then I'd look down and realize I had nearly stepped into a canyon. If Jon hadn't been there to navigate, I would probably have taken a billion hearts of fall damage by now. We kept walking on and on like that for a while until we reached a place with a lot of dirt mounds. I saw a little pink head peek over one of the mounds and look at me. I smiled, and the little pig looked frightened until Jon waved from on top of my shoulder. The little pig then smiled at Jon, and then at me. We had made it to the camp of the villagers that weren't taken.

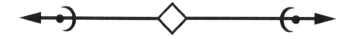

7.

PIG – IT TAKES A VILLAGE

BERNARD AND I HAD FINALLY REACHED THE REFUGEE camp, and I was glad to see so many familiar faces. There were friends and family there, and also some of the soldiers I had fought with during the invasion of our village. Even though I explained that Bernard was there to help, they were all still a little uneasy, though they were trying hard not to show it.

"Say there uh... Bernard was it? Anyway, do you really think you can help us get rid of the wolves? I mean, I know you're strong, but trust me when I say these wolves are strong too."

said Thomas, who was a pig soldier. It was the obvious first question. When I left, the entire village had been hoping that I'd come back with a small army of elite, well armed soldiers. Bernard was impressive, but he wasn't an army. That's what they thought, anyway.

Bernard went to stand up to go grab the tree pencil he had ripped out when we got there, but he couldn't because of the swarm of piglets that had been playing on him since I told them he was a gentle giant. They'd been climbing up and down, treating him like a walking jungle gym. At first he was nervous because he didn't want to accidently hurt any of them, but now he was laughing with them. Bernard loved that he could make people happy instead of scared; I could see it in his eyes.

Anyway, that meant that he wasn't paying that much attentions to the questions that the villagers were launching at him, so most of them I answered for him.

"Bernard is more capable than an army. In the human village, the iron Golems protect the city at night from the monsters. Bernard here defeats four or five of them a night, sometimes more. We're in good hands, don't worry." I said, and it seemed to put most of the villagers at ease. "Anyway, he and I both need some rest. We've been travelling all night to get here, and we'll be of more use if we have a good day's sleep. Is there anything else we should know?" I asked. There was an elder pig that approached us this time. They had little gray hairs on top of their pink head, and their ears sagged, showing their age. They hadn't been in the battle, or at least I hadn't seen them before today. The village was small, but it wasn't that small.

"Yes young man, there is. There were some scouts that we sent to the valley on the other side of the mountain, and they came back with some rather interesting reports. Apparently, there are as many are thirty wolves in our little town. There are only ten warrior pigs left to go with you and your big friend here. Whatever you decide to do, and however you decide to do it, remember this; there were more of us than them in the first fight. They captured nearly all of our warriors. They have us outmatched in terms of strength and speed. And to make matters even worse, we only have a single night to free all of their prisoners before the full moon. When you wake up and the sun goes down, the clock will be ticking. I wish you the best of luck because, honestly, you'll need it, both of you." The elder pig walked away slowly and then laid down in one of the small dirt dwellings they had made as a temporary shelter.

The old man was incredibly right. We were outmatched. But that was before we had Bernard. Maybe we could do it. Maybe, just maybe, we could win. I walked over to Bernard and tapped him on the knee.

"Come on buddy, we need to get our rest." I said. Bernard said goodbye to all the baby piglets, and they all dashed away laughing and smiling and waving goodbye back to him. Bernard yawned loudly, so loudly in fact that I had to shout at him to be quiet for fear that the wolves would hear him.

One thing was for sure; the wolves would never see him coming. I bet they didn't even know about the existence of iron Golems, just like the pigs. We would have the element of surprise on our side, and it would make all the difference in the world.

Bernard and I settled down on the outskirts

of the camp. Bernard was fast asleep almost as soon as he closed his eyes. The poor guy had a rough night, it was no wonder. Is the sun came up, and I walked into one of the underground shelters to sleep, I looked over at Bernard one last time.

"Thank you Bernard. You've given this village of pigs something we haven't had since the wolves came. You gave us a chance. Sleep well big guy." I said quietly, and then I yawned and lay down. Even though I fell asleep quickly enough, I still couldn't help but think about Hazel, and how she must be feeling scared and alone up there in that tower. I would save her; there was no doubt about it.

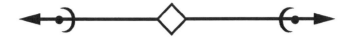

8.

Iron Golem – The Battle Begins

I WOKE UP IN THE LATE AFTERNOON AT TWILIGHT, JUST before the sun had completely fallen out of the sky. I looked over in Jon's shelter made of dirt, but he wasn't there. I walked over to the main part of the camp, and noticed that all the baby pigs were in bed asleep. I missed getting to play with them, but I knew they needed their rest, so I didn't wake them up.

I saw Jon standing over by a crafting table in the center of town. There was a single pig

standing beside him who was finishing up something.

"Oh, there he is. My name's Fredrick and you must be the famous iron Golem I've been crafting my fingers off for. Bernard, right?

You're every bit as impressive as the elder said. Glad to meet you! I'm just finishing up on the project I've been working on since your arrival. You're just in time to try it on." Fredrick said. I smiled at him, but he seemed kind of... odd to me, even for a pig. He tossed me four silver items, and I opened my inventory and put them on.

When I had all four pieces on, I realized what I was wearing. I had seen a few humans wear armor before, but I'd never put on any myself. In fact, I'd never seen anyone other than human wear armor before.

"It's a full suit of iron! It took all the rest that we had taken with us when we fled from the village, but I think it'll be worth it. How do you feel?" Fredrick asked me. I looked at him a smile of gratitude. "Perfect!" Frederick exclaimed.

After that, we joined a small group of pigs who had large iron swords in their mouths. They looked a little silly, but they used a piece of wood to test their skills, and boy, were they fierce. They gripped the handle in between their teeth and turned their necks hard enough to swing it. One fighter actually destroyed a log with a single swing. It was quite impressive.

"Alright, everybody gather 'round. Here's our strategy. The main goal of this mission is to rescue all of the pigs at the top of the mountain, okay? Our best chance of doing that is to be direct. We might not be able to take out all of the wolves, but if we can avoid most of them, we should be safe. Bernard will clear a path straight up the mountain, and you all will follow close behind. When we get to the top, all we need to do is clear out any guards and then take the captured pigs back down the mountain and head for the human village. The rest of the villagers are already on their way as we speak. If we do this right, we can be stealthy and the majority of the wolves won't even know the prisoners were rescued until tomorrow night on the full moon. By then, we'll be long gone. Are there any questions?" Jon said. None of the other pigs said anything. The plan was very straight forward. There were no unnecessary risks, but there was no backup plan either. This had to work. "I know that you all are here because you volunteered, but I have to ask one more time. If you are unsure about this, you can still leave with the rest of the village. This will be a dangerous mission, and no one would blame you if you left." Jon said. He scanned across the faces, and all of them looked determined. Finally, he looked at my face, and I tried to have the same look of confidence that the pig warriors did. "Well okay then. Let's move out!" Jon said. He hopped on my shoulder, and with that, we were off.

Jon and I were at the front of the pack. The mountain wasn't very steep, but that just made it all the slower of a climb because we had to move when we had plenty of cover. The element of surprise was our weapon. Without it, the sheer number of wolves would be enough to overpower us.

We came across out first pair of wolves about a third of the way up the mountain. They were vicious looking creatures with huge fangs and jagged looking gray fur. We hid and avoided them until they moved on, then started making out way back up the mountain. The closer we got to the top, the more regularly we'd see groups of four or five wolves walking together at a time. By the time the top was near, it was inevitable that we'd be spotted.

The wolf that spotted us actually didn't see us; he saw our footprints in the dirt, specifically mine. He followed the trail back with three others and there was no choice but to fight.

The first charged at me without thinking, and then the moment he saw me he turned with his tail between his legs and tried to run. He saw one of the pigs and tried to take them out, but the pig was too quick with the sword and destroyed the wolf after a short struggle. I noticed that the wolves mostly attacked with their razor sharp teeth. The next wolf charged at me, but he had a friend close behind. I guess he had gotten over the shock of seeing me because he was quickly on me before I had a chance to react. The wolf behind him followed suit, and it was all I could do to hold them back away from Jon. They bit down into my metallic arm, and whined as they hurt their teeth on the

iron armor. I took some damage, but not as much as they did. Before they could let go, I flung them off as hard as I could. One of them flew a good distance and then was taken down by the fall damage. Sadly, the other one landed on his feet and began sprinting to get back up. Some of the pig warriors wanted to go chase the wolf down but Jon knew it was too late.

"Wait! We have to give it up now, there's no time. As soon as they get back up we're done for! Just rush to the top, it doesn't matter if we're seen. Let's move!" Jon shouted. He was right, we needed to get there now or our goose was cooked.

I kicked off the ground and used my momentum to force myself up the mountain. I was well ahead of the pig warriors in no time at all. I could see the outline of the prison where the pigs were being kept. There was a small flattened clearing just in front of it. I jumped to there from a rock just below it, and landed with a resounding boom. I looked over at the prison, and could see the pig's faces from between the bars. They were confused until they noticed Jon, and then they were smiling and cheering.

They grew silent when a creature padded onto the green grass. It was a wolf, but it wasn't ordinary. It was huge, almost as big as I was. Its fur was standing on end like it had been electrocuted, but its eyes were calm. It was wearing blue armor. I thought about it a moment, and recalled where I'd seen that shade of blue before. Diamond. Suddenly, I understood why the humans would run. I understood why they were always afraid. I was looking at a creature that was stronger than I was, and, for the first time in my life, I was scared.

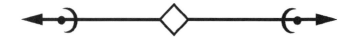

9.

PIG – IS THIS THE END?

THAT WOLF WAS BAD NEWS; I COULD FEEL IT IN MY gut. The diamond armor was insane. I thought that Bernard's iron armor was the first of its kind. I guess we never had the element of surprise.

The wolves really couldn't speak, but they did communicate with each other. I figured that this growling, snarling giant would have called in reinforcements, but he was just staring at us intently.

"Bernard, we need to end this now. If we don't beat this guy, everyone's done for, our village, the human village... everyone. If all the wolves get armor, they'd be unstoppable. We have to stop this." I said. Bernard nodded, and gave me a look of confidence, but in his eyes I could tell he didn't think this would be easy, even if it was possible.

The wolf wasn't interested in wasting any more time. He charged at us head on, fangs bore back. I gripped my necklace and braced for impact. When the wolf hit, at first I thought that Bernard had successfully stopped him. I opened my eyes and looked. To my horror, the wolf had its huge mouth gaping wide open... at me! The wolf must have seen me talking to Bernard and thought that I was giving him orders or controlling him! He was after me, and Bernard was just barely able to keep the jaws from slamming closed on me. I jumped off of Bernard and took a bit of fall damage. Bernard then slammed the wolf onto the ground, but the wolf was hardly faced. Its diamond armor seemed to take the moonlight and reflect it out even brighter. It was fierce and beautiful at the same time.

I took out my sword, but the wolf moved so fast that my eyes couldn't keep up. Bernard was fighting harder than I'd ever seen him fight, and the scary thing was, I think he was losing. It seemed like he was so much stronger when he fought the creeper in the village. Ever since we left the human village, he's been weaker than normal. I tried to think about what could have changed, and how I could help Bernard, but the longer I took, the more he was getting bashed around. Then it hit me. Bernard had his flower when he fought the creeper, that's what changed!

The wolf had its front paws pinning Bernard to the ground. Its claws came out and made an awful noise as they scraped against the metal armor. If I was going to do something, it was now or never. I opened the iron box, and instantly a warm red glow shot out. It was literally warm, and when my snout got in the way, I felt like I was being cooked. I shined the light on Bernard, and the look of pain left his face. In its face was something far more reassuring; Bernard was confident.

The wolf was distracted by the glow just long enough for Bernard to slam his hands into its side. The armor absorbed most of the damage, but a hit was a hit, and Bernard was able to stand back up.

The more light from the poppy flower that

Bernard absorbed, the faster and stronger he became. I jumped back up on his shoulder and held the box against him so all the light was hitting him. Bernard went in for a crushing blow, and made contact with the wolf's mouth. A single fang flew over and down the side of the mountain, hitting rocks and crashing wildly to the bottom. The wolf seemed to be disheartened, but only for a moment. After that, he was pure rage.

The wolf pounced on top of Bernard and knocked him over, which then sent me flying backwards. I rolled a long way before coming to a crashing stop. I took a lot of damage, and I could tell Bernard did too. From this distance, the light from the flower was too weak to really help Bernard, so he was pinned to the ground again after a brief final struggle. I ran and climbed as quickly as I could to get back on the platform, but Bernard was too far away for me to help him. Out of the corner of my eye I could see the sun rise. A new day was dawning, and I didn't know if Bernard or I would be around long enough to see it. All of the hopes of the pigs were in our hands, and here we were, letting them slip between our fingers.

Then, the sunrise got brighter. Too bright. Its red glow was unnaturally strong. Eventually, even the wolf took notice. It stepped off of Bernard and walked to the edge of the platform. From there, he could see all over the valley.

I walked to the edge and looked over. The light was coming from poppy flowers, five of them beside five iron Golems. Each iron Golem had someone holding the flower, two of them were human, and the other three were pigs. I turned to the wolf. He was growling viciously, but his tail was sinking lower and lower the closer the iron Golems came to the mountain.

The wolf leaned back on his hind legs, arched his back, and then howled at the sky. It was piercing and loud, but it also sounded defeated. He was signaling a retreat! In the fading darkness rose the sounds of the wolves as they passed the message of defeat onwards. I ran back over to Bernard as quickly as I could, and checked to see if he was okay.

"We did it... together." He said, this time clearer than he's ever spoken. I turned my head quickly, remembering that the wolf hadn't actually been defeated yet, but when I looked, he was gone.

I released the pigs, and one by one they filed out. The last to exit the prison cage was Hazel. She looked distraught and a little shaken, but she would be fine after a few days rest. I introduced her to Bernard, and though it took a little convincing, they warmed up to each other after all.

Finally, we all met there together. Bernard and I stood side by side, and we were cheered on by the crowd. Humans and iron Golems and pigs all mixed up together, all smiling and happy. It made me smile, and gave me hope. There was a small knowing at the back of my mind, though. The wolves were still out there. They could... no, they would come back. The difference now is, we'll be ready. This time, we won't be alone. And that makes all the difference.

End Vol. 1

I hope you enjoyed Diary of an Iron Golem & His Pig. If you did, we hope you will take a moment and give us a review. It tells me, "you want more" and to keep writing these wonderful adventures! It also helps others to find and experience them as well.

Diary of a Iron Golem and His Pig Vol. 2 Biome Conflict, Is next in this series! Check it out today!

We also have a great surprise waiting for you at ChristopherCraftBooks.com